ZONDERkidz

I Can Read!™

BEGINNING
1
READING

Jesus Loves the Little Children

pictures by Janee Trasler

Jesus loves the little children,
all the children of the world.

4

Dear Parent:
Your child's love of reading starts here!

Every child learns to read in a different way and at his or her own speed. You can help your young reader improve and become more confident by encouraging his or her own interests and abilities. You can also guide your child's spiritual development by reading stories with biblical values and Bible stories, like I Can Read! books published by Zonderkidz. From books your child reads with you to the first books he or she reads alone, there are I Can Read! books for every stage of reading:

SHARED READING
Basic language, word repetition, and whimsical illustrations, ideal for sharing with your emergent reader.

BEGINNING READING
Short sentences, familiar words, and simple concepts for children eager to read on their own.

READING WITH HELP
Engaging stories, longer sentences, and language play for developing readers.

READING ALONE
Complex plots, challenging vocabulary, and high-interest topics for the independent reader.

ADVANCED READING
Short paragraphs, chapters, and exciting themes for the perfect bridge to chapter books.

I Can Read! books have introduced children to the joy of reading since 1957. Featuring award-winning authors and illustrators and a fabulous cast of beloved characters, I Can Read! books set the standard for beginning readers.

A lifetime of discovery begins with the magical words **"I Can Read!"**

Visit www.icanread.com for information on enriching your child's reading experience.
Visit www.zonderkidz.com for more Zonderkidz I Can Read! titles.

Jesus said, "Let the little children come to me.
Don't keep them away. The kingdom of heaven
belongs to people like them."
—*Matthew 19:14*

Jesus Loves the Little Children
Copyright © 2008 by Zondervan
Illustrations copyright © 2008 by Janee Trasler
Adapted from the lyrics written by Clare Herbert Woolston

Requests for information should be addressed to:
Zonderkidz, *Grand Rapids, Michigan 49530*

Library of Congress Cataloging-in-Publication Data

Jesus loves the little children / pictures by Janee Trasler.
    p. cm. -- (I can read! Level 2)
  ISBN-13: 978-0-310-71620-4 (softcover)
  ISBN-10: 0-310-71620-9 (softcover)
  1. Jesus Christ--Juvenile literature. 2. Jesus Christ--Songs and music--Juvenile
     literature. 3. Children's songs. I. Trasler, Janee.
  BT302.J5734 2008
  232--dc22

                                                        2007034332

Editor: Betsy Flikkema
Art direction & design: Jody Langley

Printed in Hong Kong

08 09 10 11 12 • 5 4 3 2

Fast and funny, bold and bright,

all are precious in his sight.

Jesus loves the little children
of the world.

Jesus calls the children dear,

"Come to me and never fear,

for I love the little children
of the world."

"I will take you by the hand,
lead you to the better land,
for I love the little children
of the world."

Jesus loves the little children,

all the children of the world.

Tall and silly, kind and shy,

all are sparkles in his eye.

Jesus loves the little children
of the world.

Jesus is the Shepherd true.

And he'll always stand by you,

for he loves the little children

of the world.

He's a Savior great and strong,
who'll protect you from the wrong,
for he loves the little children
of the world.

Jesus knows the little children,

all the children of the world.

From China to Peru,

all are special, just like you.

Jesus knows the little children
of the world.

I am praying, Lord, to you
that you'll tell me what to do,
for you love the little children
of the world.

I will love my fellow friends,
and be faithful to the end,

for you love the little children

of the world.

Jesus loves the children,

all the children of the world.

From a mountain, farm, or town,
Jesus never lets us down.
Jesus loves the little children
of the world.

Jesus Loves the Little Children

Je - sus loves the lit - tle chil - dren.

All the chil-dren of the world. Fast and

fun -ny bold and bright, all are pre-cious in his sight. Je - sus

loves the lit - tle chil - dren of the world.